TO GRACE — C.L.

FOR MY OTHER HAMSTER HALF, CYNTHIA — D.A.

Text copyright © 2014 by Cynthia Lord
Illustrations copyright © 2014 by Derek Anderson
All rights reserved. Published by Scholastic Press, an imprint of Scholastic Inc., *Publishers since 1920*.
SCHOLASTIC, SCHOLASTIC PRESS, and associated logos are trademarks and/or registered trademarks of Scholastic Inc.

ISBN 978-0-545-67814-8
10 9 8 7 6 5 4 3 2 1       14 15 16 17 18
Printed in U.S.A. 08
First edition, April 2014

The display type was set in Ziggy ITC and Coop Black.
The text was set in Cochin Bold, Gill Sans Bold.
The art for this book was done in acrylics.
Book design by Marijka Kostiw

# Hot Rod Hamster

## MONSTER TRUCK MANIA!

By
**Cynthia Lord**

Pictures by
**Derek Anderson**

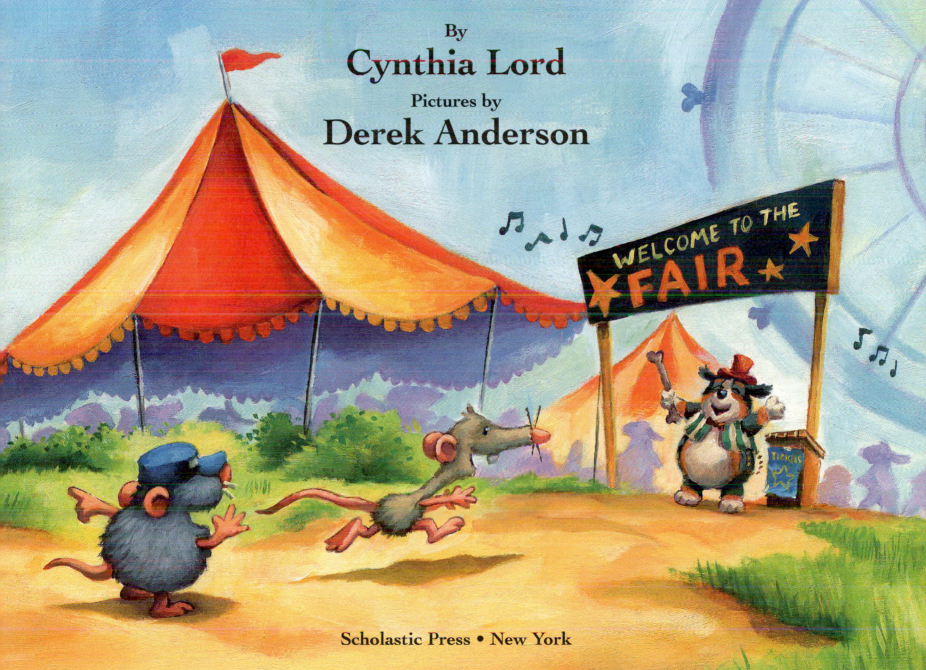

Scholastic Press • New York

Truck day, treat day, cotton-candy sweet day.
Fun day, fair day, music in the air day.

Sailboat, rowboat, pirates long ago boat.
Sub boat, tugboat, chugga-chugga-chug boat.
Which would *you* choose?

Plain cup, bright cup, checkered black-and-white cup.

New cup, old cup, rimmed in shiny gold cup.

**Which would *you* choose?**

Sports car, race car, fun in outer space car.
Cop car, mail car, make the siren wail car.
Which would *you* choose?

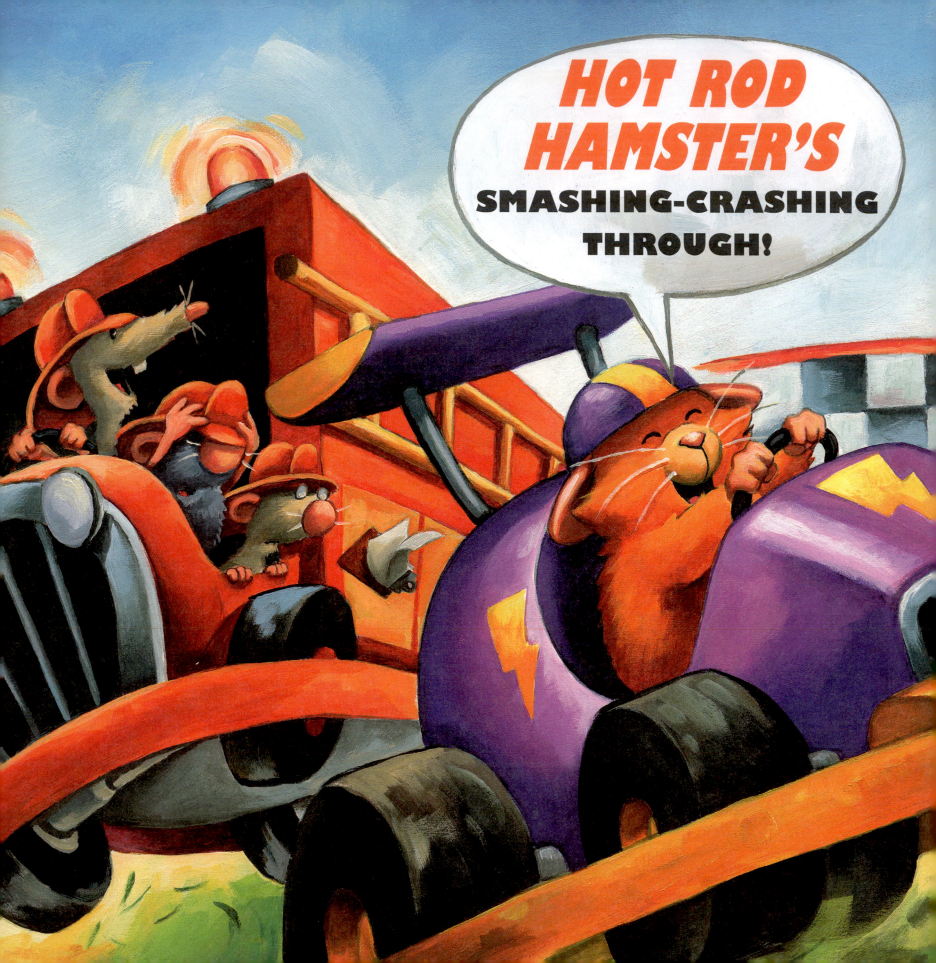

Red swirl, peach swirl, mix a bit of each swirl.

Blue swirl, green swirl, tasty tangerine swirl.

Which would *you* choose?

Huge truck, high truck,
mud is gonna fly truck.
Strong truck, steel truck,
make those tires squeal truck.

Hot treats, cold treats, wrapped in pretty gold treats.
Slurp treats, lick treats, eat it on a stick treats.
**Which would *you* choose?**